I0672590

FIELDS OF GOLD

William Fucilla

Published 2011 by arima publishing
www.arimapublishing.com

ISBN 978 1 84549 499 5
© William Fucilla 2011

All rights reserved

This book is copyright. Subject to statutory exception and to provisions of relevant collective licensing agreements, no part of this publication may be reproduced, stored in a retrieval system, or transmitted in any form or by any means, without the prior written permission of the author.

Printed and bound in the United Kingdom
Typeset in Palatino Linotype, 12pt

This book is sold subject to the conditions that it shall not, by way of trade or otherwise, be lent, re-sold, hired out, or otherwise circulated without the publisher's prior consent in any form of binding or cover other than that which it is published and without a similar condition including this condition being imposed on the subsequent purchaser.

In this work of fiction, the characters, places and events are either the product of the author's imagination or they are used entirely fictitiously. The moral rights of the author have been asserted. Any resemblance to actual persons, living or dead, is purely coincidental.

Swirl is an imprint of arima publishing.
arima publishing
ASK House, Northgate Avenue
Bury St Edmunds, Suffolk IP32 6BB
t: (+44) 01284 700321
www.arimapublishing.com

Dedication

I dedicate this book to my love, Anya Edwards, for her inspiration, affection and belief in me.

This book was written in loving memory of her mother, Denise Tutt.

The author and his girlfriend, Anya Edwards, in New York City, 2007

Scene 1

INT. CONCENTRATION CAMP - NIGHT

Credits open to the sounds of militant marching.

Cut to the boots of German soldiers marching through a concentration camp. They halt and turn to unlock a door; they begin to select prisoners, some of which include women and children. Some of the women have been so severely deprived of food that their bones look as if they will perforate through their frail skin. The anonymous soldiers begin to strip them down.

Camera on a young man, Elliot Levi. He looks on in horror, at the surrounding events, as the sounds of women and children, shrieking and crying resonate around the camp.

Cut to a woman providing some resistance by holding her child tightly, refusing to strip, to preserve her dignity and honour. Her child is pulled away and she is struck to the ground. Her head thumps against the floor.

Cut to the child screaming.

Camera on a malnourished old man who is being stripped. He is exhaling and inhaling extremely deeply, and can barely stand up. Elliot watches on in dismay, feeling a great sense of guilt as he is helpless and cannot come to the aid of the prisoners.

Cut to a dimly lit corridor. People are being led outside by the soldiers to the "Little White House". Fear and horror has consumed these innocent souls as they walk up to the isolated location. As they exit the door, the freezing conditions penetrate through their naked bodies.

Cut to a long shot of these oppressed people walking towards the "Little White House", which is ahead in the distance. Loud barks of the SS officer's Alsatians are heard.

Cut to German Officers loading them into the gas chambers. The maximum capacity of the "shower room" has been greatly surpassed, and they are almost being stacked upon one another. The door is locked behind them; the sounds of screams and cries are heard throughout the room, in anticipation of their grim fate. The smell of death seems to linger around this dwelling.

Cut to the commanding officer of the camp, Wolfgang Biermann.

WOLFGANG

(Callously) **Release them**................ *(In German: Subtitles in English)*

Camera on the inside of the chamber. People are screaming and rushing around frantically in complete disarray. Solid pellets of Zyklon B are dropped into the chamber; and cyanide gas is dispersed around the room.

Camera pans out of the room and moves away from the gas chamber. This is simultaneously accompanied by the sound of the gas and screams. The outside scenery is now seen. The camera continues to pan into the corridor where they exited the building. The camera pans all the way down the corridor which led these individuals to their execution. The screams gradually become softer and softer as the camera moves further down the dimly lit corridor, however the sound of gas remains the same. The screen goes black, but the sound of gas is still heard.

Cut to the next scene.

Scene 2

INT. MAGGIE'S KITCHEN - DAY

Scene opens to the sound of gas, which is emanating from a stove.

Camera close up on the gas cooker. Fire sparks from it. A pan containing oil is placed on top, and an egg is cracked into it. As the egg hits the object, crackling sounds are heard.

Cut to a middle-aged mother, Maggie, who is preparing breakfast for her eighteen year old son. She sighs in frustration, turns around and walks towards the stairs.

MAGGIE

Robby...... How many times do I have to tell you....................Come down, breakfast is ready........

ROBBY

Hold on, just a sec.

MAGGIE

Come on, we're going to be late.

Cut to a close up of Maggie. Cut to the next scene.

Scene 3

INT. MAGGIE'S CAR - DAY

Camera on Robby in the passenger seat of the car. He is listening to his I-pod, as he refutes to listen to Magic fm. He is also reading the latest addition of FHM.

Cut to a side shot of Maggie and Robby in the car. Maggie is trying to get his attention.

MAGGIE

Robby....... Robby......

She looks over to him, but he fails to acknowledge her.

Close up of Robby. His music is loud enough to burst his eardrums, and he is completely consumed by his own inner thoughts.

Camera cuts to a semi-nude model, on the page of the magazine.

Cut to a side shot of Robby and Maggie.

MAGGIE

Robby............... Robby...............

There is still no response. She reacts by pulling his headphones out of his ears.

Camera on Robby. He turns abruptly.

ROBBY

(Agitatedly) **What! What is it?**

Camera on Maggie from Elliot's perspective.

MAGGIE

(Sarcastically) **Well it would be nice to talk to your son, once in a while.**

Camera on Robby. He is looking in complete disgust. He is clearly not an enthusiast of this type of music.

ROBBY

Well, turn this crap off and I'll talk.

Camera on Maggie. She immediately reacts by turning off the radio.

MAGGIE

Fine.

Maggie has a cheeky smirk on her face.

MAGGIE

Happy now?

Cut to Robby. The adolescent rolls his eyes and sighs.

ROBBY

(Half heartedly) **Yeah.**

Robby closes his magazine.

ROBBY

Ma, how long is it till we get there?

Cut to Maggie.

MAGGIE

About another ten minutes.

Camera on Robby. He yawns and looks out of the window.

Cut to the sun shining on the beautiful, golden cornfields.

Cut to a shot of Robby from outside the car window, gazing at the picturesque scenery which surrounds them.

Camera on the fields from Robby's perspective.

Cut to Maggie. She briefly turns her head to look at them.

Cut to the cornfields.

MAGGIE

Isn't it just beautiful?

Cut to a close up of Robby. He is still fixated on the cornfields and has been utterly captivated by them. He nods his head in agreement and smiles.

Cut to an overhead shot of the car and a sign saying "Welcome to St. Christian's Hospital".

Camera on the car moving away.

Cut to the next scene.

Scene 4

INT. HOSPITAL- DAY

Camera on Robby and Maggie, entering the hospital, via automatic sliding doors. They walk over to the reception.

Camera on the lady behind the desk, who smiles.

Camera on Maggie.

MAGGIE

Morning. We're here to see Elliot Levi......

Cut to the receptionist. She methodically searches him on her database, and then turns towards them, providing Maggie with a pen and form.

RECEPTIONIST

Could I kindly ask you to fill out this visitor's form, please?

MAGGIE

Sure no problem.

She fills it out and hands it back.

Camera on the receptionist.

RECEPTIONIST

Thank you. He's on the second floor, in the Cardiac Unit.

Camera on Maggie and Robby.

MAGGIE

Thank you.

Robby acknowledges the receptionist by smiling at her. Robby and Maggie walk off.

Cut to next scene.

Scene 5

INT. HOSPITAL - DAY

Camera on the lift opening.

Camera on Maggie and Robby getting out of it.

Cut to them walking down the long, brightly lit corridor. The sun rays shine through the windows onto the white hospital walls.

Camera cuts to them stopping by the main desk, for the cardiac unit. Maggie leans over. The man behind the desk points to the door.

Cut to a door opening. Maggie and Robby walk in.

Cut to an old man (Elliot Levi) laying on the bed. His head is turned and he is looking out of the window.

Camera on the heart monitor. It shows that his heartbeats are abnormally slow.

Cut to Elliot. Maggie walks towards him.

Cut to Maggie from Elliot's perspective. She holds his hand.

Camera on the old man. He looks up, diverting his attention towards Maggie. He smiles.

ELLIOT

(Softly and contently) **Maggie..........**

Camera on Maggie. She smiles whilst caressing his hand.

Camera on Elliot.

ELLIOT

And how is my favourite niece?

Camera on Maggie.

MAGGIE

I'm fine. And you?

Cut to Elliot. He smiles.

ELLIOT

(Jokingly) **As well as an old timer like me can be.**

Cut to Maggie who smiles.

Cut to Robby, from Elliot's viewpoint. He walks over and then stops beside his mother.

ROBBY

Hey uncle El.

Cut to Elliot.

ELLIOT

Ah... Robby. Looking well son. Nice to see you.

Camera on Robby.

ROBBY

Thanks Uncle El.

Camera on Elliot.

ELLIOT

Help yourselves to some drinks; there's water and orange juice over there.

Camera on Robby who walks over to the beverages. He turns around before pouring the water.

ROBBY

Ma, do you want anything?

Camera on Maggie and Elliot. She expresses her refusal by shaking her head.

Cut to Robby.

ROBBY

Uncle El???

Camera on Maggie and Elliot. Maggie pulls up a chair, to sit beside Elliot.

ELLIOT

Water please.

Camera on Robby. Maggie explains how Elliot's other nieces; Ruth and Sarah will be coming tomorrow morning, as it was the earliest flight they could get. Whilst they are talking, Robby gets a cup from the window sill, to pour Elliot a drink of water and once again he is mesmerized by the golden fields outside.

Close up of Robby gazing at the cornfields.

Cut to a shot of the cornfields from Robby's perspective.

ELLIOT

Beautiful hey?

Robby awakes from his hypnotic state. He looks over to Elliot.

ROBBY

Yeah.

He then walks over and places the cup on Elliot's tray.

Camera on Elliot. He turns his head away from the window and looks at Robby.

ELLIOT

Thanks son.

He has a sip of the water and then places it on his tray.

Camera on the trio. Robby pulls up a chair to sit next to them.

Cut to Elliot staring out of the window, continuing to look out at the majestic fields. He is smiling, but yet his facial expressions also convey melancholy.

Camera on the fields from Elliot's perspective. The wind is blowing on the crops, causing them to dance in a sequence.

Cut to a close up shot of Elliot. He is staring intensely at the cornfields. A tear emerges and rolls down his cheek.

Camera on Robby and Maggie. They are both concerned. Maggie moves towards him.

MAGGIE

Uncle..... Are you ok?

Camera on Elliot. He swallows and breathes out in order to keep his emotions intact.

Cut to a shot of the trio. The camera pans towards them.

ELLIOT

It was a day just like this in the summer of 1944..........

The camera pans towards the window and then out onto the golden cornfields.

Cut to the next scene.

Scene 6

EXT. CORNFIELDS - DAY

Camera long shot of cornfields and a little cottage, located at the top of them.

The credits read *"Bohemia and Moravia, 1944."*

It's a scorching hot day, with temperatures reaching up to the mid 30s.

Camera on a young, native woman, Rose. She is carrying a basket as she gracefully walks towards the washing line ahead. Rose's white dress, as well as the garments hanging out to dry are swaying backwards and forwards, manipulated by the gusts of wind.

Rose stops by the line, placing her basket on the floor. She begins to remove the pegs and places the clothing in the basket.

Cut to a shot of a young man (Elliot Levi). He has been doing various types of manual labour and is clearly fatigued from the day's work. He stretches out his arms and then sits down on the steps outside his home.

Camera on Elliot gazing over towards Rose. He is enthralled by her angelical figure.

Camera on the golden crops ahead in the distance, from Elliot's view. They are being swayed by the breeze.

Camera close up of Rose. She turns around almost telepathically sensing Elliot's stare. She momentarily stops her activity and smiles at Elliot.

Cut to Elliot. He reciprocates the gesture by smiling back.

Camera on Rose, who turns and resumes taking down the clothes.

Cut to Elliot who gets up and walks into the house.

Camera on him inside the humble dwelling. He stops and picks up a picture of him and Rose.

Cut to the photo.

Camera close up of Elliot. He smiles, puts the photo down, gets a cold beer and caresses it across his forehead. As he cracks open the bottle of cold beer, sounds of tanks are heard.

ROSE

(Shrieking) **Elliot!!!!!!!!!**

Camera on Elliot, who drops the beer bottle. It smashes on the floor. The trepidation has manifested itself in his eyes. He sprints towards the door.

ELLIOT

(Screaming) **Rose!!!!! Rose!!!!!**

Cut to Elliot running down the steps. He sees German soldiers holding onto Rose.

Camera on Rose and two soldiers. They drag her along the ground towards a tank, whilst she frantically attempts to get them off her.

ROSE

(Hysterically) **Help! Help me. Please somebody!!!!**

Camera on Elliot. He runs towards her.

ELLIOT

Get off her!!

Camera on Elliot who is confronted by another two soldiers. They body check him and then pin his arms by his sides. Elliot manages to liberate one of his arms and throws a punch at one of them. The aggressor hits the ground due to Elliot's powerful right hook. However the other soldier quickly reacts by head butting Elliot. He falls to the ground in a daze.

Cut to Elliot laying on the floor from the view of the soldier standing over him. Rose's screams are heard. The German's shadow has completely eclipsed Elliot's body.

Cut to a shot of the soldier from Elliot's perspective. He rams the back of his Gewehr 41 rifle into Elliot's face. The screen blacks out.

Cut to the next scene.

Scene 7

INT. FREIGHT CAR - NIGHT

Cut to a shot of Elliot's face. His eyes are opening and shutting, as he tries to regain consciousness.

Cut to a longer shot of Elliot. The perspiration has drenched his top, and he has a great degree of sweat on his face. He is sitting up with his back against the door of a freight train, tightly sandwiched in between people. His eyes are fixated on the floor. Suddenly he awakes from his lethargic state due to the strong stench of urine, faeces and decaying corpses. He begins coughing violently and almost vomiting.

Cut the camera to a bucket load of faeces with flies buzzing over it.

Camera on a rotting dead body.

Camera on the other passengers. The vehicle is so overcrowded that there is virtually no room to move. The internal humidity and temperature has reached soaring heights.

Camera on Elliot, whose loud coughs awake some other people laying and sitting around. Among them is a bearded, Jew, Elijah Ehrenbaum. He appears to be withdrawn and physically exhausted.

Camera on Elijah who is sitting opposite Elliot.

ELIJAH

(Jokingly) **You'll have to excuse the smell.**

Camera on Elliot who looks around perplexed and fearful.

Camera on some gypsies sleeping.

Cut to Elliot turning his head.

Camera on some other Jews from Elliot's perspective.

Cut to Elliot. He exhales deeply and tries to gather his thoughts. He looks at Elijah.

ELLIOT

Where's Rose?

Cut to Elijah.

ELIJAH

Who?

Cut to Elliot.

ELLIOT

(Stuttering/ agitated) **Mm..mm..mm..my wife. Rose......**
Where is she?

Cut to Elijah.

ELIJAH

They must have separated you guys.

Camera on Elliot. He becomes more upset and
disconcerted. It seems that he has repressed the events of

the abduction and is experiencing some form of cognitive dissonance.

ELLIOT

*(Shouting/ perturbed)***Who separated us!!!!**

Camera side shot of Elliot and Elijah. Elijah moves towards him.

ELIJAH

(Calmly) **Just calm down.**

Camera on Elijah. He pushes his hands down and then elevates them repeatedly, similar to the motion of a yo-yo. He tries to contain Elliot like a psychiatrist tries to tranquilize a mental patient.

Cut to Elliot looking squarely at Elijah.

ELLIOT

(Uncontrollably) **I'm not calming down! Rose??? Rose????**

Camera on Elijah placing his hands on Elliot's shoulders forcefully.

Cut to some of the gypsies and other passengers awaking and viewing Elliot's frenzy.

Camera on Elijah. He is holding Elliot and shaking him.

ELIJAH

(Loudly/ Authoritatively) **Look calm down...... Just calm it....**

Camera on Elliot who appears to be more composed.

Cut to the duo.

ELIJAH

(Commandingly) **Don't lose your head. We all need to be strong and united. You've got to be calm...... Or you've got no chance.**

Elliot calms down after a commanding speech from Elijah. The duo stare at each other intensely and then shake hands.

Camera on Elijah.

ELIJAH

Elijah.

Camera on Elliot.

ELLIOT

Elliot.

Camera on the two of them and the surrounding passengers.

Camera cuts to Elliot staring at Elijah.

Cut to Elijah who looks back at his newly found friend.

Cut to Elliot. He continues to look at Elijah.

YOUNG ELLIOT: NARRATION

He was a great man..... Resilient.

Camera on Elijah trying to get some sleep.

YOUNG ELLIOT: NARRATION

Nothing fazed him. Seemed like no matter what life threw at him, he was prepared for it.

Cut camera to old Elliot laying in his hospital bed, whilst Maggie and Robby listen on.

OLD ELLIOT

He was captured a few days before me. He explained how he had been travelling for days in these inhumane conditions, trapped in a confined space..... The journey was somewhat as bad as the destination. The smell and sight of dead bodies decaying around us...........

Cut back to Elliot in the freight car, his eyes are open and his facial expressions are emotionless.

YOUNG ELLIOT: NARRATION

It was the longest ride of my life. Not knowing where Rose was...... If she was even still alive.... But the worst of it was the realisation that our toughest test was yet to come.............

Camera pans out of the train.

Camera pans to an overhead shot of train. Thunder is heard and bolts of lightning light up the night sky like a fireworks display. Ahead in the distance, awaits the main entrance to the Auschwitz-Birkenau concentration camp.

Cut to the next scene.

Scene 8

INT. FREIGHT CAR - DAY

Camera on Elliot who is asleep.

Suddenly the door is opened and penetrating rays of light shine through. Elliot awakes abruptly; he is squinting due to the intensity of the sun rays. It is around 4 o'clock in the afternoon.

Cut to German soldiers ordering the people to get off the train and head towards the platform.

Cut to Elijah. He walks over to Elliot.

Camera on Elijah and Elliot. Elijah helps Elliot get up. They then exit the train.

The new prison inmates are welcomed by growling German Shepherds and the grotesque smell of disease and dead bodies. The fumes from the crematorium linger in the air.

Cut to Elliot. He is halted by two soldiers.

Camera on Elliot and the soldiers. They begin stripping Elliot, removing all of his personal belongings and leaving them on board the train. His shirt is thrown back in the freight car. This was a customary procedure and was a means to deindividuate the prisoners.

Cut to Elliot's arm. One solider grabs it and removes his wedding ring from his finger, throwing it into the train.

Camera close up of Elliot. He is clearly aggrieved and feels a sense of humiliation.

YOUNG ELLIOT: NARRATION

They stripped us of our clothing and of our dignity............

Camera on Elliot who is now completely nude.

Cut to one of the soldiers, nodding his head, indicating that Elliot can resume walking towards the platform.

Camera on the crowds of newly transferred inmates and German soldiers. There are thousands of naked people present, most of them being; Jews, gypsies, Poles and Soviet prisoners. Like a herd of cattle they are forced upon the railway platform by the SS officers and their dogs.

Camera on Elliot amongst the masses of people.

Cut to a shot of Rose in the crowd of people ahead, from Elliot's perspective. Elliot sees her.

ELLIOT

(Loudly) **Rose!**

Rose turns.

Cut to Elliot. He is waving his arm to get Rose's attention and trying to get passed the other prisoners.

Camera on Rose. He catches her attention. Her eyes instantly light up and for that split second nothing in the world appears to matter. The strength of their love seems to transcend all the sorrow and torment which is imminent. She moves towards him.

Camera on the duo passing through the crowd to get to one another.

Cut to them meeting. The undressed couple hug tightly and kiss.

ELLIOT

I love you.

Elliot rests his forehead on the bridge of her nose. They are deeply fixated on one another.

ROSE

(Subdued and Terrified) **I love you too.**

A tear rolls down her cheek. Elliot kisses her forehead.

ELLIOT

We're going to get out of here Rose I promise you. Yeah......

Rose nods her head while she tries to remain composed and control her tears and inner anguish. The sounds of crying children and mothers reverberate around the station. The couple turn their attention to a Jewish family.

Camera on a Jewish father, Sam, refusing to let go of his; wife, little son and daughter. Two officers grab the man and force him to let go of his children.

SAM

Get off me!

The officers fling him onto the floor.

Camera on his wife and the children shrieking and crying. Sam's wife tries to run towards him but is inadvertently obstructed by the masses of people.

Camera on Sam. He gets up trying to get back to his wife and kids, but he is blocked by the two towering and menacing figures.

Camera on Sam and the two soldiers.

SAM

Sarah!

He speculatively attempts to evade the two officials. They grab him and try to restrain him.

Camera close up of one of the officers.

GERMAN OFFICIER

(Threateningly) **Just calm down.....** *(In German: Subtitles in English)*

Cut to a close up of Sam. He continues to try and liberate himself from their overpowering grasps, as he knows that his kids and wife will probably be deemed useless to the Nazis, and immediate execution is extremely probable. The Germans throw him on the floor out of frustration.

Cut to Sarah moving towards him.

Cut to Sam attempting to get up and break through the colossal figures. However, as he does this one of the generals shoots him right in between the eyes.

Camera on Sarah who sprints over to her deceased husband. She drops to her knees.

SARAH

(Screeching) **Noooooooooooo! No. No......God!**

Her piercing laments resound around the platform and amidst all the noise and chaos; this innocent woman's cries are heard clearly.

Cut to Elliot. He buries Rose's head in his chest to protect her from viewing the scenes.

Camera on Rose. Her eyes expand to full capacity as she is clearly disturbed by these tyrannical and barbaric events. Her heart rate accelerates as she is fully aware that the future is ominous. In addition this scenario has understandably petrified the other prisoners and this is evidently an example of the consequences of trying to circumvent the Nazi rules and commands.

Camera on the officer that shot Sam. He grabs the widow by her hair, brutally dragging her away from her dead spouse.

Camera on her children who are also violently moved away from their father.

Camera on Rose and Elliot. They are also separated with force by other officers who in their opinions are trying to create order, in this anarchic environment. The ubiquitous sense of fear, sorrow and despair continues to grow and spread across the outside of the camp like a malignant cancer.

Cut to Elliot. His eyes follow Rose as she is escorted away by officers.

Cut to Rose walking away. Her eyes are still fixated on Elliot. The young lovers are distraught. This monstrous abode, synonymous with evil and despair awaits them. Rose's vibrancy and vivaciousness appears to have been drained.

Camera on the officers. They begin allocating the prisoners into two separate lines.

Cut to mostly; women, children, the disabled, old and weak men being sent to the left hand file. The other file comprises of the young, fit and healthy.

Cut to Elliot being pushed by an officer into the right side. Elliot is looking around concerned as he is unable to find Rose.

Camera close up of Elliot's face.

YOUNG ELLIOT: NARRATION

The left hand side was for mostly woman, children, the old, the disabled and the unhealthy.................... If you were in that line, you were queuing to meet your maker. And there was nothing you could do about it....... Not knowing if Rose was in that queue made it even worse.

Camera on Elliot looking over at a young mother with her son.

Camera on the mother and son.

Cut to the little boy, who is holding his mother's hand. He is staring back at Elliot innocently; completely unaware of what is to come.

Cut to Elliot. He diverts his attention towards the clear blue skies above. The weather does not reflect the mood and temperament of the masses.

Camera on the sun. (Music: Secret love by Nico).

Cut to the next scene.

Scene 9

INT. CONCENTRATION CAMP - DAY

(Music continues to play). Camera on Elliot entering the concentration camp. Camera on the inmates working. The labourers are digging deep holes with shovels. The intense heat is causing some of them to pass out in the sun.

Cut to one of them dropping to the ground due to the heat and malnutrition.

Cut to the officers picking him up and coercing him to work harder. The man drops to the ground again. He is beaten with a club, due to his failure to continue.

Cut to prisoners carrying emaciated corpses to the crematorium.

Cut to Elliot turning his head. He looks towards the cells.

Camera on the overcrowded cells. The prisoners have no space or room and are kept like animals. They have shaved heads and appear to be severely starved. These images are seen in slow motion.

Cut to a dazed Elliot who looks on in sorrow and despair.

Music subsides.

Cut to the next scene.

Scene 10

INT. CONCENTRATION CAMP - DAY

Camera on lines of new inmates queuing to be registered.

Cut to Elliot he is looking ahead at the desk. His facial expressions convey complete anger.

Cut to a side shot of the queue, which is slowly going down.

Camera on Elliot approaching a conceited registrar.

Cut to the registrar who is seated and some guards, from Elliot's view.

REGISTRAR

Come forward please. *(In German: Subtitles in English)*

Camera on Elliot from the Registrar's viewpoint.

REGISTRAR

Do you speak German? *(In German: Subtitles in English)*

Camera on Elliot. He just stares into the registrar's eyes and does not respond.

Camera on the registrar from Elliot's view.

REGISTRAR

Do you speak German? *(In German: Subtitles in English)*

Camera on Elliot. He fails to reply again.

Close up of the seated German. He strokes his moustache and sniggers, while looking around at the other guards.

Camera on the other guards who smirk.

Cut to the registrar. He is concealing his transparent vexation behind his fabricated grin. The registrar nods his head to the side and indicates for the guards to deal with Elliot accordingly.

Cut to Elliot as a guard moves towards him.

Cut to a side shot of Elliot and the soldier.

Cut to a close up of Elliot from the guard's perspective.

Cut to a close up of the robust German from Elliot's view.

Cut to a side shot of the duo. They appear to be having some sort of psychological warfare. Suddenly the guard strikes him in the face.

Camera on Elliot falling to the ground.

Cut to the guards picking him up and dragging him towards the desk.

Camera on the registrar, who provides him with some clothes.

REGISTRAR

(Sarcastically) **Here you go. Easy way next time?** *(In German: Subtitles in English)*

Camera on the guards who take the clothes. They escort Elliot away from the desk. They hold Elliot up by his arms. He only has his torso and above, off the ground. Elliot is being dragged and his legs are scrapping along the terrain.

Cut to an aerial shot of the queue of prisoners lining up and Elliot being dragged away. Cut to the next scene.

Scene 11

INT. CONCENTRATION CAMP -DAY

Cut to the guards and Elliot. He is being pulled down a corridor. Either side of them are cells filled with prisoners.

Cut to shots of prisoners.

Cut to a close up shot of Elliot from behind, being dragged.

Cut to a close up of Elliot's face. He is severely fatigued, as he has not eaten for days. His lips are heavily chapped and dry due to deprivation of water. In addition he is trying to recover from the punch he received.

Cut to the guards and Elliot stopping in front of a door. They open it.

Camera on the tattooist who awaits Elliot.

Cut to the guards putting Elliot on a chair.

Cut to Elliot sitting. The guards forcefully grab his left arm and pin it down onto the table.

Cut to the tattooist placing a large stamp equipped with needles, on Elliot's inner forearm. The needles puncture his skin. Ink is then applied onto the wound, in order to complete the inscription.

Cut to Elliot. He is clenching his teeth together and he moves his head back abruptly as he is experiencing immense discomfort.

YOUNG ELLIOT: NARRATION

The tattooing was part of the registration process....... It was a way to dehumanize us. We were merely numbers to them..............

Camera on Elliot in a room getting his head shaved.

Cut to him being flung into a barrack and the door being shut behind him. He lands on his front. He turns and sits up.

Camera on Elliot's left sleeve. He rolls it down and looks at his tattoo. It reads "97370". Additionally, a triangle has been tattooed under the number sequence.

He looks around and sees Elijah amongst the inmates.

Camera on the prisoners and Elijah. They are asleep.

Camera on the guards. They open the door and provide Elliot with; a cup of water, a tiny quantity of bread and watery soup, comprising of rotten vegetables and meat.

Cut to Elliot drinking the water, savouring every drop. He starts eating the food provided to him.

YOUNG ELLIOT: NARRATION

Sometimes we'd go for days without food.............. A watery soup made up of rotten veg and meat was a real treat.........

Elliot is devouring the food. He is so hungry that he is oblivious to the fact that the food has gone off.

Cut to Elliot looking around.

Cut to Elliot looking down at the floor.

Camera on the floor. It is littered with rat faeces.

Camera on Elliot getting into bed.

Cut to Elliot looking out of a small gap, created by a structural defect.

Cut to a German guard with his Alsatian, from Elliot's view. The powerful German shepherd is seated obediently, panting, beside the guard. He is stroking the dog and expressing great love towards the creature.

GUARD

Here boy. *(In German: Subtitles in English)*

The guard throws the dog a fresh tender piece of chicken.

Cut to a shot of Elliot from the dog's perspective.

YOUNG ELLIOT: NARRATION

**They could show such affection towards an animal......
Yet they wanted us dead........**

Camera on the dog eating the food. He finishes it and then walks over to his master.

Camera on the dog and owner. He begins stroking it.

GUARD

You enjoy that boy? Yes you did. Good boy. *(In German: Subtitles in English)*

Cut to Elliot. His eyes are glazing over. Eventually he falls asleep.

Cut to the next scene.

Scene 12

INT. ELLIOT'S DREAM - NIGHT

Cut to a shot of Rose smiling at Elliot, like she did that day at the cornfields.

Cut to Rose screaming and trying to get away from the soldiers who drag her to the tank.

Cut to Elliot twitching in his sleep due to the viewing of his disturbing mental representations.

Cut to Rose saying, "I love you too" when the couple reunited at the station platform.

Cut to a shot of Rose naked in a gas chamber screaming as the gas ascends on her.

Cut to Elliot. He awakes from his nightmare. He rises into a seated position, breathing heavily and looking around the barrack. He settles down again and lies back down.

Cut to the next scene.

Scene 13

INT. BARRACKS – EARLY MORNING

It is 4am in the morning. Camera on Elliot and the other inmates asleep. They are woken up by their Kapo (an inmate in charge of the work team), Fritz, who is shouting at them.

Camera on Fritz entering the barrack.

FRITZ

(Shouting/ psychotically) **Rise and shine........ You pieces of shit..... You Yids..... Get up!!** *(In German: Subtitles in English)*

Fritz is a convicted rapist and paedophile in Germany. The obscure and distant look in his eyes sends shivers down the spine of those who meet him. He is loud, abrasive and over exuberant, belonging either in solitary confinement or a psychiatric ward.

Camera on Elliot and the others. They get up quickly, rallied by the psychotic Fritz and begin making their beds, which had to be made precisely.

Cut to the prisoners standing up in attention.

Camera on Fritz. The sadistic Kapo begins walking around inspecting the beds.

Cut to a shot of a bed. There are minor, unavoidable creases on the heavily stained blanket, which lays on top of the shapeless straw mattress.

Cut to the Kapo's club on an insignificant wrinkle.

Camera on the Kapo. An evil leer emerges on his face.

Cut to a side shot of Elliot and the inmates standing in attention. The Kapo walks along the front of them.

Camera on Fritz staring right in the face of one of the prisoners. Fritz moves along to the next detainee. He does the same and moves to the subsequent captive.

Cut to Fritz stopping in front of Elijah. Close up of the duo. They are staring at each other with a great degree of hostility. Suddenly Fritz rams his weapon into Elijah's abdomen. Elijah leans forward, making a ninety degree angle with his body. He is holding his stomach, in pain. The ruthless German begins striking him on his back, forcing Elijah to fall onto his knees. Fritz goes to administer more pain.

Cut to Elliot who turns and tries to preclude the Kapo, from beating Elijah. Fritz turns and hits Elliot across the face, causing him to fall to the ground.

Cut to Fritz. He continues to mercilessly beat Elijah.

Cut to a shot of the other prisoners. They are turning their heads and screwing up their faces, conveying utter nausea at the scenes.

Cut to Elliot on the floor. His lip is cut. He spits out some blood, whilst looking over at the beating that Elijah is receiving.

YOUNG ELLIOT: NARRATION

Everyone stood there frozen...........

Cut to Fritz hitting Elijah with the club, from Elliot's perspective.

YOUNG ELLIOT: NARRATION

Terrified that if they reacted, it would constitute immediate death........

Cut to Fritz. He stops assaulting Elijah and walks away.

Camera on Elijah. He eventually gets onto his knees, holding his midsection.

Cut to Elliot looking at him.

Cut to the next scene.

Scene 14

EXT. SURROUNDING GROUNDS OF THE CONCENTRATION CAMP - DAY

Cut to Elliot, Elijah and the others digging up the land. The large openings are made in order to bury the increasing number of murdered prisoners.

Cut to a guard on a watch tower looking around.

Camera on Elliot working away. He is sweating and straining, due to the nature of the work and the scorching conditions.

Cut to Fritz. The psychopath watches over them working away whilst he also digs.

YOUNG ELLIOT: NARRATION

Fritz was a callous and mentally disturbed individual........ Convicted of countless acts of rape and paedophilia.....

Cut to a shot of Fritz patrolling the barracks.

YOUNG ELLIOT: NARRATION

He'd patrol the barracks late at night......

He stops and gazes lustfully at a teenage captive, who is asleep.

Cut to a shot of the girl sleeping.

YOUNG ELLIOT: NARRATION

Preying like a hawk on young girls...........

Cut to Fritz entering the barrack. His eyes light up at the sight of the young, virginal girl. He removes his shirt.

Cut to Fritz watching over the workers.

YOUNG ELLIOT: NARRATION

He was a monster, devoid of reason or compassion........
He made life hell for those around him..............

Cut to an aerial shot of workers labouring intensively.

Cut to Elliot digging.

YOUNG ELLIOT: NARRATION

Days were long and hard..... The only thing which kept me stable and going in these hellacious surroundings was Rose..... My thoughts always diverted to her...... The mere possibility of seeing her again acted as my adrenaline....... I had to keep going.......

Camera close up of Elliot, who is reminiscing about the past. He has a flashback.

Cut to Elliot walking through the cornfields, as the sun is beginning to set. Juxtaposed to his current state, Elliot looks fresh and full of vitality. He is holding a bag of bread. As he approaches his house, he stops and turns to look at the cornfields.

Camera on the idyllic scenery. Rose sneaks up on him.

Cut to a shot of Elliot staring at the picturesque surroundings. Rose puts her arms around him from behind, catching him by surprise.

Cut to a close up on Rose and Elliot.

ROSE

(Sexy/Cheekily) **And where have you been all my life???**

ELLIOT

The bakery.

The couple laugh. Elliot turns and they cuddle. The lovers are staring at each other provocatively.

ELLIOT

(Cheekily) **And where have you been all my life???**

ROSE

*(Cheekily)***You know. Just here..... Cooking........**

They smile at each other. Elliot lifts her up and she wraps her legs around his waist.

Close up of them kissing.

He gently lays her down on the fields and places the bag of bread beside them.

They stop kissing. Elliot moves his index finger along her bountiful lips.

Cut to Elliot from Rose's perspective. He is totally captivated by her beauty.

Camera on Rose from Elliot's view. Her luscious long, golden locks are spread along the terrain. She sweetly gazes back at Elliot. Her eyes sparkle like that of a manga characters, conveying her purity and innocence.

Camera on Elliot fixated on Rose. Rose puts a crop in Elliot's ear and tickles him. Elliot awakes from his reverie. He glances to the side and sees the crop.

Cut to Rose who laughs.

Camera on Elliot who looks back at her, he laughs and begins to tickle her neck, in order to get some playful revenge.

Cut to Rose who appears to be extremely ticklish in this area. She is pushing her chin down towards her chest, in an attempt to prevent Elliot from tickling her.

ROSE

(Laughing) **Stop it......**

Elliot just continues.

ROSE

(Hysterically/ Laughing) **Stop it......**

With her free hand she grabs Elliot and engages in some horseplay with him.

Cut to the couple rolling along the cornfields, laughing and joking with one another.

Cut to Rose laying on top of Elliot. The couple calm down and start kissing again. Elliot then moves his head back to admire the goddess above him.

Camera on Rose from Elliot's view, who is smiling at him.

Cut to Elliot in the concentration camp. He has momentarily stopped digging and is in a world of his own.

Cut to Elliot and Fritz. The Kapo is standing in front of him.

FRITZ

(Shouting) **Get back to work!!** *(In German: Subtitles in English)*

Elliot is revived from his daydream and begins working under Fritz's command. Fritz walks away.

Cut to Elijah and Elliot. Elijah is excavating the turf and is clearly frustrated and cannot endure this intense labour. He has bruising around his right eye and several cuts on his face.

ELIJAH

Don't know how much more of this shit I can take.......

Elliot looks at him.

ELLIOT

My friend, we are in this for the long haul........

Cut to Elijah.

ELIJAH

(Sarcastically) **And I used to complain about the sound of my wife's nagging voice................ Geeze. I'd welcome it with open arms right now.**

Cut to Elliot who smiles at his joke.

ELLIOT

You sure about that one Eli???

Camera on Elijah who chuckles.

ELIJAH

You've got a point there.

Cut to Elijah. He elevates his shovel which has a large quantity of earth on it.

He pauses and looks at Elliot.

ELIJAH

Thanks for having my back, back there...... I appreciate it........

Elijah throws the residual terrain off the tool, displacing it to the side.

Cut to Elliot.

ELLIOT

No probs.

Elliot briefly stops his activity. He looks over to Elijah.

ELLIOT

(Confidently) **We've got to be united and strong. Right?**

Cut to Elijah smiling. Cut to the next scene.

Scene 15

INT. BARRACKS - NIGHT

Cut to Elliot laying on his bunk bed staring at the ceiling.

YOUNG ELLIOT: NARRATION

Elijah and I were fortunate to some extent......... Our jobs consisted of some manual labour, transporting dead bodies and sorting out the clothes of dead prisoners...........

Cut to one of the inmates, Steven. The twenty year old is respiring extremely poorly, and is holding his chest. He coughs up some blood.

YOUNG ELLIOT: NARRATION

Others were sent to work in the mines or gas factories. Most contracted deadly lung disorders due to the fumes and pollution....... And when you'd passed your sell by date that was it..................

Cut to Elliot. The sounds of militant boots hitting the floor are heard, along with Steven's whizzing. Elliot's eyes shift as the presence of two men draw nearer.

The door of the barrack is opened. The visitors move towards the prisoners, their shadows cover Elliot's body.

Cut to Fritz and Gerhardt Fuhrmann, one of the SS officers.

Cut to a shot of Steven who is breathing terribly.

Cut to Fritz. He is looking at the weak, homosexual, Jew, whose breathing seems to be deteriorating by the second. Fritz has a big smirk on his face and is in utter ecstasy.

He starts shaking Steven.

FRITZ

Get up! You little faggot! *(In German: Subtitles in English)*

Cut the camera to Steven, experiencing severe discomfort. He is looking up at Fritz and Gerhardt, helplessly and refuses to get up.

Cut to Fritz. He violently pulls up Steven by his ears.

FRITZ

Get up!!! *(In German: Subtitles in English)*

The euphoria that Fritz is experiencing, equates to the amount of jubilation he feels when he ruthlessly rapes innocent woman and children. The victim's breathing becomes even more laboured.

Cut to Gerhardt intervening. He presses his club against Fritz's midriff to stop him from going into a frenzy and beating Steven.

GERHARDT

Hey!! None of that! *(In German: Subtitles in English)*

Cut to Elliot watching on.

Camera on Fritz and Gerhardt. Fritz has momentarily stopped taunting and abusing Steven, under the stern commands of Gerhardt.

Cut to Steven from Fritz's view. Steven is seated, as Fritz attempts to remove his clothing. He makes a feeble attempt at preventing Fritz from taking off his garments.

Camera on Fritz who is becoming increasingly agitated by Steven's efforts.

Cut to a side shot of the two wrestling.

FRITZ

*(Screaming)***Stay still dam it!** *(In German: Subtitles in English)*

They continue to struggle. Fritz's vents his anger by clubbing him to the head. Steven falls to the ground. The savage unsavourily spits on Steven.

GERHARDT

Hey!!!!! *(In German: Subtitles in English)*

Cut to Gerhardt. The stout German grabs the heartless delinquent and pushes him against the wall. Gerhardt puts his club up against Fritz's neck, consequently causing Fritz's breathing to become severely restricted.

Cut to a close up of Gerhardt and Fritz. Gerhardt is incensed by what he has just witnessed.

GERHARDT

I told you to stop! You disobey my orders again, I'll kill you! Do I make myself clear? *(In German: Subtitles in English)*

Gerhardt applies a little less force. Fritz has that distant look in his eyes; he is smiling and finds the situation hilarious. Gerhardt responds by putting more downward pressure on the weapon, thus limiting Fritz's air supply to a greater degree.

GERHARDT

Do I make myself clear?!! *(In German: Subtitles in English)*

Fritz is frantically tapping the club, indicating to Gerhardt that he cannot breathe. Gerhardt holds the lock for another few seconds and then stops, letting go of Fritz.

Cut to a shot of Fritz and Gerhardt from Elliot's view. Fritz is smiling and looking down at Steven. Gerhardt shoves him towards the door.

GERHARDT

Get out of here you sick bastard. *(In German: Subtitles in English)*

Fritz leaves.

Cut to Gerhardt. He walks over to Steven.

Camera shot of Steven on the floor. Gerhardt helps him up.

Cut to a shot of Steven on his feet. The young man has succumbed to his inevitable destiny. He has a graze on his face, and begins to snivel as Gerhardt commences stripping him down.

Cut to a shot of Gerhardt. He is looking at Steven, with an ice cold look in his eyes.

Camera on Steven, whose shirt is now off. Tears begin streaming down from his eyes like a waterfall.

Cut to Gerhardt.

YOUNG ELLIOT: NARRATION

He was the epitome of pragmatism and authority. He had a job to do, and he saw it through, in a typical Germanic fashion.

Camera shot of Steven weeping like a two year old.

Cut to a shot of Gerhardt. He has a controlled look on his face. The German appears to be unfazed.

Cut camera to Steven whose underwear is removed. He continues to cry.

Cut to a close up of Gerhardt. The sternness of his stance and facial expressions remains.

YOUNG ELLIOT: NARRATION

But behind that austere facade, laid a sentimental and highly emotional individual......

Cut to a shot of naked prisoners being escorted to the "Little White House".

Cut to the doors being sealed.

Camera on Gerhardt standing in attention outside the gas chamber. The sounds of gas and screaming are heard. A tear drops from his eye and he swallows, causing his Adam's apple to move. This is done to contain his emotions. He quickly wipes the tear off his face, as he sees Wolfgang approaching him.

Cut to Wolfgang, who stops by Gerhardt. He has a large grin on his face, feeling a sense of triumph.

WOLFGANG

Great job my brother. We are making, He and our nation proud.

Cut to Wolfgang and Gerhardt staring at each other. The leader grabs one of Gerhardt's arms, shaking it victoriously.

Cut to a shot of Gerhardt who nods.

Cut to Wolfgang walking away.

Camera close up of Gerhardt. The oppressed man, is acting against his free will, and thus feels a great sense of bitterness and grief.

Cut to a shot of the soldiers walking away. The sounds of the gas and shrieks are still heard.

Cut to a shot of Elliot resting in the barrack.

The sounds of gas and yelling lowers.

YOUNG ELLIOT: NARRATION

From that day on...... I realised..... Hell did exist..... And it wasn't in the afterlife. It was here.......... Dante had only ingeniously depicted to us, a highly artistic and censored version of it in "The Divine Comedy"....

Cut to a shot of Wolfgang Biermann, walking into his office.

YOUNG ELLIOT: NARRATION

And there he was...... Wolfgang Biermann, Satan himself. Commanding it all from the ninth circle.

He undoes his shirt and pours himself a glass of whiskey.

Cut to him sitting snugly in his chair, drinking his alcoholic beverage. He seems to be delighted with today's work.

YOUNG ELLIOT: NARRATION

He was the personification of evil....................

Cut to him staring at the wall in front of him. He is looking at it like a man possessed.

Cut to a propaganda poster of Hitler.

YOUNG ELLIOT: NARRATION

Blindly obsessed and brainwashed by His notions...... He endeavoured to ensure that the final solution would be seen out.

Cut to Wolfgang looking up at the advertisement, in total awe of it. He is looking at the image of Hitler, as if he were in the presence of God himself.

Cut to a shot of Elliot in bed looking up at the ceiling. The sounds of crickets are heard. He opens his watch and checks the time.

YOUNG ELLIOT: NARRATION

Two Weeks, three days, six hours and twenty-three minutes, since I last saw Rose. I stayed up every night thinking about her... Awaiting the day I'd see her again. It's incredible what love can make the human spirit endure.... For it was the only thing giving me the will to live.

Cut to a shot of Rose in the cornfields smiling.

Camera on Elliot laying in his barrack.

YOUNG ELLIOT: NARRATION

I just hoped my journey through hell, would somehow lead me to her..........

Cut to the next scene.

Scene 16

INT. CONCENTRATION CAMP/RECREATIONAL AREA
- NIGHT

The scene opens to Wolfgang and officers playing cards. They are casually sitting around; drinking whiskey, laughing and joking.

Cut to a German informer, Karsten, who enters the room. He marches briskly towards Wolfgang. He salutes him.

Camera on Wolfgang. He pulls up a chair for him.

WOLFGANG

Karsten, here take a seat..... *(In German: Subtitles in English)*

Wolfgang leans over the table to get the bottle of whiskey. He picks it up.

WOLFGANG

Have some whiskey..... You look tense my boy. *(In German: Subtitles in English)*

Camera on Karsten.

KARSTEN

No thank you Sir. *(In German: Subtitles in English)*

Cut to a close up of Karsten and Wolfgang. Karsten moves closer towards him to whisper something in his ear.

KARSTEN

(Whispering) **Can I speak to you alone outside please?** *(In German: Subtitles in English)*

Camera on the officers around the table. Wolfgang appears to be slightly tipsy.

WOLFGANG

Whatever it is you want to say, you can say to all of your fellow countrymen.... *(In German: Subtitles in English)*

Close up of Wolfgang. His eyes are bloodshot.

WOLFGANG

Please speak my boy..... *(In German: Subtitles in English)*

Camera on the group who continue playing, but the noise levels have completely diminished.

Camera on Karsten who is standing.

KARSTEN

As you will Sir. *(In German: Subtitles in English)*

Camera on the group around the table and Karsten.

KARSTEN

Sir. You recall that group of Jewish mine workers that were reported missing, for three days, around four weeks ago? *(In German: Subtitles in English)*

Camera on Wolfgang who is clearly alerted.

WOLFGANG

(Worriedly) **Go on......** *(In German: Subtitles in English)*

Cut to Karsten.

KARSTEN

Sir. They are alive and well back in Hungary. *(In German: Subtitles in English)*

Cut to Wolfgang. In a schizophrenic rage he slams his glass on the table.

Camera on everyone around the table. They are all silent.

Cut to Karsten.

KARSTEN

(Hesitantly) **Sir all the deportation of the vermin has ceased from Budapest..... Officers; Arensdorf, Diefenbach, Heidbrick....... Dead. The word is spreading Sir........** *(In German: Subtitles in English)*

Arensdorf, Diefenbach and Heidbrick were pivotal figures in the transportation of the Jews from Hungary to Auschwitz.

Cut to Wolfgang. He stands up in a wild outburst of anger, partly due to the news and some credit is owed to the influence of alcohol. He stumbles on his feet and grabs Karsten by his collar.

The other officers get up and try to alleviate the tension.

Camera close up on Wolfgang and Karsten. Gerhardt separates them.

Camera on Wolfgang. He is standing near the corner of the room after being restrained.

WOLFGANG

(Angrily) **You are all a disgrace, to your countrymen, and to Him. How did those rats get away! You all did your jobs properly none of this would have transpired.....** *(In German: Subtitles in English)*

Camera on Gerhardt. Wolfgang pushes him and shapes up to attack him.

Camera on the others creating a physical division between the two.

Cut to Wolfgang back in the corner.

WOLFGANG

Our fellow brothers have been killed because of those merciless vermin. They were great men and will die as martyrs. *(In German: Subtitles in English)*

Camera on the officers watching Wolfgang's rant.

Camera on Wolfgang.

WOLFGANG

(Quietly) **Imagine if they could see this now? I assure you they would be turning in their graves. I tell you now you give these rats scraps.... Beat them till they are black and blue..... Make them suffer. And if you see one of them trying to escape...............** *(In German: Subtitles in English)*

Wolfgang chuckles callously.

WOLFGANG

(Callously) **You bring it to me and we execute it publicly! Making sure we let it die a slow and painful death...........** *(Shouting)* **Is that understood?!** *(In German: Subtitles in English)*

Camera on the silent officers. They are being coerced to agree to Wolfgang's demands.

Cut to Wolfgang. He picks up the bottle of whiskey, walks to his office door and opens it. Subsequently, he slams the door shut and drinks a large quantity of whiskey from the bottle. He then wipes his mouth and sits in the chair.

Cut to a shot of the heavily intoxicated leader, staring at the poster once again.

Cut to the poster of Hitler.

Cut to the next scene.

Scene 17

INT. BARRACKS – EARLY MORNING

Cut to a shot of Elliot sleeping.

FRITZ

Rise and shine animals. *(In German: Subtitles in English)*

Cut to Elliot squinting, due to a torch light being shone on his face.

YOUNG ELLIOT: NARRATION

And that was the best part of the day...... Getting woken up by a psychotic, rapist, paedophile, who we didn't understand.

Camera shot of Fritz devouring a chicken wing, while holding a flashlight in his other hand.

Cut to Elliot looking in disgust and putting his hand over his eyes to shield himself from the incisive beam.

YOUNG ELLIOT: NARRATION

And the cycle started all over again...............

Cut to a shot of Elliot outside with Elijah digging the terrain.

Camera on Elliot and Elijah carrying frail dead bodies to the pits which they had dug up.

YOUNG ELLIOT: NARRATION

Most of the bodies were sent to the crematorium..... Some were left in reserve, so the sick fucks could allocate us these jobs to gratify their sadistic fantasies.

Cut to Elliot dropping to the floor, exhausted. He begins vomiting due to the sight, disgusting odour and handling of the corpses.

Cut to Fritz walking over to him. He boots Elliot in his abdomen.

FRITZ

Get up! You pussy......... *(In German: Subtitles in English)*

Camera on Elliot he tries to rise up to his feet but he gets kicked to the floor again.

Cut to Elliot in a laundry room, scrubbing clothes.

Camera on Elliot folding garments.

Cut to Elliot walking down a corridor towards the storage room for clothes. He pauses and looks at the area on the other side, which is separated from his section by barbed wire.

Camera on some women, sewing.

Camera on Rose.

Cut to a shot of Elliot whose eyes light up.

YOUNG ELLIOT: NARRATION

And there she was. Although she was severely fatigued and looked a few pounds underweight...... She still had that radiance.

Camera on Elliot moving towards the wired fencing.

ELLIOT

Rose....

Camera on Rose who looks up surprised. She puts her hand over her full bodied lips, which begin to tremble.

ROSE

(Overjoyed/ Teary) **Oh my god. Elliot?**

Rose gets up and runs towards him.

Camera on the couple. The barbed wired creates a physical division between them, however they are holding hands through the gaps. Rose is crying.

ROSE

(Shuttering/ amazed) **You're still alive...... I missed you so much......**

Camera on Elliot who looks teary too. He holds her hands even tighter.

ELLIOT

I've missed you too baby...... Been thinking about you every night.

Cut to Elliot who turns his head as he hears Fritz's voice. Elliot realises that he has to stop the discussion and continue his work. Elliot turns to face Rose.

Camera on Rose and Elliot.

ELLIOT

(Whispering) **Look you meet me here every day at 2 o'clock.........**

Rose nods her head.

ELLIOT

I gotta go baby..... I love you.

ROSE

I love you too.

Rose walks away.

Camera on Fritz and Elliot. The young Jew has the clothes in his hands, and is being followed by Fritz.

Cut to a close up shot of Fritz from the other side of the barbed wire. He pauses staring at the women sewing. Brutal sexual images are running through his perverse mind.

Cut to Elliot in the storage room.

YOUNG ELLIOT: NARRATION

She was alive. Hope is such an indefinite notion..... Yet hope was taking me far.......... I now knew for sure that I had to keep going.

Cut to the next scene.

Scene 18

INT. CONCENTRATION CAMP - DAY

Scene opens to Elliot and Rose meeting by the barbed wire area.

Camera on Elliot.

ELLIOT

Here I got you something.

Cut to a shot of Elliot's hand going through the gap in between the wires. He is holding a dandelion.

Camera on Rose. She smiles at him and looks down at it.

Cut to Elliot.

YOUNG ELLIOT: NARRATION

Wow, the look in her eyes when I gave her it. It was like I gave her a pot of gold.

Cut to Rose.

ROSE

It's beautiful. Thank you.

Cut to the couple.

ELLIOT

You ok baby?

Cut to Rose.

ROSE

15 hour days of; sewing, scrubbing the clothes of guards. Up early hours, no rest, little food......... How can I be...?

Rose becomes emotional and starts crying.

ROSE

(Traumatized) **Watching women being stripped down..... Night after night........ Some go straight there. Some get raped and beaten before..........**

Cut to a distressed Elliot.

Cut to Rose.

ROSE

When they enter..... My heart stops....... Wondering am I gonna be next....... Death and destruction is all around us Elliot...... I can't stand it anymore...... I just can't.

Cut to Elliot.

ELLIOT

(Reassuringly) **Baby. Listen to me very carefully, ok??**

Cut to Rose who is snivelling.

Cut to Elliot.

ELLIOT

**Listen to me Rose. We are going to get out of here, ok?
Don't give up Rose. You're a fighter, I know it Rose.
Don't give up.**

Cut to Rose regaining her composure.

ROSE

I better get back to work.

Camera on Rose walking away.

Cut to a close up of Elliot, watching her walk away. He has
tears in his eyes.

YOUNG ELLIOT: NARRATION

Seeing her like that just broke my heart. I had to be strong for both of us.

Cut to old Elliot laying on his hospital bed. He has tears in his eyes.

Camera on Maggie and Robby comforting their uncle. Maggie wipes the tears from his eyes with a tissue.

OLD ELLIOT

Thank you.

Elliot pauses.

OLD ELLIOT

We met every day at two o'clock without fail.

Cut to a side shot of Elliot, Robby and Maggie. The camera moves towards the window behind them. The sun is setting over the cornfields.

OLD ELLIOT

The months went by.

Camera on the golden cornfields outside.

OLD ELLIOT

Summer was over.

Cut to a shot of Auschwitz concentration camp, in the winter. The snow is falling heavily.

YOUNG ELLIOT: NARRATION

And the harsh oppressive winter set in.

Cut to a shot of individuals arriving at the train station. They are stripped naked and herded like cattle towards the platform.

Cut to long lines of people waiting to be registered. They are unbearably cold.

YOUNG ELLIOT: NARRATION

The people that queued for days didn't make it.........
They froze to death.

Cut to dead bodies in the snow being dumped in a pit.

Cut to Elijah on the bottom bunk.

ELIJAH

Elliot we gotta get the hell out of here.

Camera on Elliot on the top bunk.

ELLIOT

You crazy? It gets down to minus ten at night out there.....
If we lose our way, we are sure to freeze to death......

Cut to the two of them. Elijah gets up and looks at Elliot.

ELIJAH

What damn choice do we have? We've gotta take that chance. Sooner or later we are going to die in here anyway.

Camera on Elliot.

ELLIOT

Yeah. And when we get out the surrounding villages are filled with them..... That's if we make it that far! There's no guarantee the soldiers and their dogs won't find us in the woodlands. We'll stick out like a sore thumb. Three Hebrews with B.O....... Two with shaved heads in striped pyjamas. Great idea Eli!!!!

Cut to Elijah.

ELIJAH

(Sarcastically) **Yeah you're right let's stay here...... And just wait to die. I'd rather be dead right now anyway. So as far as I'm concerned we got fuck all to lose trying.**

Cut to Elijah going to lie back down.

Cut to Elliot.

YOUNG ELLIOT: NARRATION

At first the possibility of an escape seemed far too risky..... But suddenly, it dawned on me.

Cut to the next scene.

Scene 19

EXT. GROUNDS OUTSIDE THE CONCENTRATION CAMP - DAY

Camera on Elliot doing his standard daily chore of digging.

Cut to Elliot stopping and focusing on something.

Cut to a shot of a woodpile.

Camera shot of Elliot.

YOUNG ELLIOT: NARRATION

We'd been working on the grounds surrounding the camp for several weeks now, as they were ominously constructing more barracks, in anticipation of more prisoners.......

Cut to Elliot and Elijah moving timber.

Cut to the prisoners finishing their work at night.

Cut to a SS officer doing a role call in order to check that no-one was missing.

YOUNG ELLIOT: NARRATION

**We knew from previous experiences that searches for missing prisoners lasted up to three days max.........
Rumours had it, that some got away and it was causing uproars between officers in the camp..... We knew the risks of getting caught.....**

Cut to a flashback of a man getting publicly hung.

Cut to Elliot in his barrack.

YOUNG ELLIOT: NARRATION

The odds were stacked against us..... But I had to get Rose and I out of here..........

Cut to Elliot and Elijah talking to their fellow inmates.

YOUNG ELLIOT: NARRATION

We explained our plan to the others. They co-operated with us, however none of them had the guts to actually escape...........

Cut to Elliot and Elijah talking and shaking hands.

YOUNG ELLIOT: NARRATION

We had the plan all mapped out in our minds.......... In theory it was simple. We would be working on the surroundings grounds like any other day.

Camera on Elliot, Elijah and the others working.

YOUNG ELLIOT: NARRATION

When the turnover for watch guards took place we'd hide in the woodpile.

Cut to a shot of the guards swapping over.

Camera on Elliot and Elijah entering the woodpile and the other prisoners laying wood on top of the opening.

Cut to everyone finishing the days work and queuing to enter the camp.

Cut to Elliot and Elijah enclosed in the woodpile.

YOUNG ELLIOT: NARRATION

Then on the third evening, when the search stopped........... We'd make a run for it.

Cut to Elliot looking at his watch inside the woodpile.

Cut to them getting out.

Camera on the duo running through the woodlands at night.

Cut to Elliot laying down in the barrack.

YOUNG ELLIOT: NARRATION

The only thing that was a problem was how Rose was going to fit into this scheme. We somehow needed to get her into the construction area.

Cut to the next scene.

Scene 20

INT. CONCENTRATION CAMP - DAY

Camera on Rose. Elliot has just propositioned her about the getaway.

ROSE

(*Whispering*) **El... I don't know..... It sounds too risky to me.....**

Cut to Elliot. He recalls how one of Rose's occupations was to clean the clothes of the SS Helferin (the female guards).

ELLIOT

(*Whispering*) **Here me out. You have access to the guards' uniforms right??**

Cut to Rose who nods her head.

Cut to Elliot.

ELLIOT

(Whispering) **Right...... Tomorrow, during the day, take one of the uniforms and hide it in the bathroom.**

Cut to Rose carrying the clothing to the bathroom.

ELLIOT

At exactly six forty-five go back to the bathroom and change into the guard's uniform.

Cut to Rose in the bathroom, wearing the guard's uniform.

Cut to Elliot.

ELLIOT

At that time the guards will do a role call and realise, Eli and I are missing.

Cut to a roll call being conducted.

Camera on a guard realising that two inmates are not present. He is enraged.

Cut to a shot of the chaos and disarray amongst the guards.

Cut to a shot of Auschwitz II main entrance. Guards begin to vacate the premises expeditiously, searching the surrounding areas in their entirety. Most of them are accompanied by dogs.

Camera on the guards and their dogs in the woodlands.

Cut to Rose walking down the corridor in her disguise.

ELLIOT

(Whispering) **At this point. You leave the bathroom.......
Find your way around to the woodpile and join us.**

Cut to Rose outside, approaching the woodpile. She then gets in it.

Cut to Elliot who continues explaining the plan.

ELLIOT

(Whispering) **We wait till the search is called off on the third day, then we make our move...........**

Camera on Rose. She nods her head, signifying her agreement to the proposal.

Cut to Elliot who smiles.

Cut to the couple kissing through a gap in between the wires, which separates them.

Cut to Rose walking away from Elliot's perspective.

Cut to Elliot. He watches her walk away.

Cut to Elliot lining up for a role call. Another day's work on the construction site has come to an end.

Cut to Elliot gazing up at the starry night's sky.

ELLIOT

It was all set. Everyone knew their role........ Our fate was in our hand's.......

Cut to a shot of the sky. The night turns into dawn.

Cut to the next scene.

Scene 21

EXT. NEW CONSTRUCTION SITE - DAY

The scene opens to the inharmonious sounds of Kapos and guards shouting orders at the prisoners.

Cut to a shot of Elliot moving some planks of wood. He is the quintessence of concentration and is continually running over the scheme in his mind.

Camera on the guard in the watch tower looking around.

Camera close up of Elliot who is looking at Elijah.

Cut to Elijah staring back. The two of them are displaying complete focus. They are fully aware of what they have to do.

Cut to Elliot staring back.

Cut to the next scene.

Scene 22

INT. CONCENTRATION CAMP - DAY

Scene opens to Rose walking towards the storage room for clothes. She has just left the laundry room. She has her head down and is trying not to attract attention to herself.

Cut to female guards conserving with one another, as Rose passes by them.

Cut to Rose. She continues walking down the corridor.

Camera on a pile of clothing in Rose's hands. In the middle of the pile, concealed by the prisoners' garments is the SS Helferin uniform. Rose enters the toilet.

Cut to a shot of Rose kneeling in front of a toilet in the corner of the room. Guards continue to walk passed.

Camera on the clothing. She quickly removes the top half of the garments and places the SS uniform behind the toilet.

Cut to Rose leaving the sanitary room, with the remaining clothes.

Cut to the next scene.

Scene 23

EXT. NEW CONSTRUCTION SITE - DAY

Camera on the watch tower guard looking over at his replacement. His back is facing the workers.

Cut to a worker who is being lazy and refusing to work.

Cut to Fritz who walks over to him. His attention is completely focused on the indolent labourer.

FRITZ

Work you Yid fuck! *(In German: Subtitles in English)*

Cut to Elliot swiftly climbing into the woodpile, with the assistance of other inmates, while Fritz beats the reluctant worker.

Cut to Fritz beating the inmate.

Cut to Elijah who enters the woodpile. The other workers lay the blanks of timber on top of the stack to hide the duo.

Camera on the watchman turning and facing the workers.

Cut to a shot of the woodpile.

Cut to the next scene.

Scene 24

EXT. NEW CONSTRUCTION SITE - NIGHT

Cut to a shot of the prisoners finishing their day's work at the new construction site, from Elliot's perspective. He is viewing this through a small gap in the woodpile.

Cut to the guards leading the inmates to the camp entrance for a role call.

A guard begins to tally up the numbers against his sheet.

Cut to a shot of the guards and prisoners from Elliot's perspective. The guard, who is counting up the detainees, is infuriated. He rushes off to inform the others.

Cut to a shot of Elliot and Elijah peering through the gaps, observing the scenes.

Cut to a shot of the guards running around the concentration camp, frenetically. They are preparing to carry out extensive searches.

Cut camera to Rose in her disguise, moving quickly towards the exit. While she is doing this there is severe instability within the camp, guards are scurrying around, and dogs are barking viciously.

Cut to a shot of the entrance of the camp. Guards are rushing out, being pulled along by their grossly agitated Alsatians.

Cut to a shot of the guards looking around the woods. The dogs are sniffing around, trying to ascertain where Elliot and Elijah are.

Cut to Rose at the exit moving away undetected.

Cut to Rose approaching the stack of wood. She is fully aware that guards are scrutinising every segment of land and are trying to notice any suspicious behaviour.

Cut to Rose by the pile. She looks around.

Cut to a shot of a guard in the distance flashing his light around Rose's proximity.

Cut to Rose quickly hiding behind the stack of timber.

Camera on Rose slowly moving her head towards the side of the pile, to see whether the guard has departed.

Cut to Rose. Half of her head is hidden behind the adapted dwelling. She is scanning the location of the guard with one eye.

Cut to the flashlight being shone near Rose. Rose screens herself behind the wooden structure.

Cut to the guard being called away by another officer.

Cut to the two officers walking away.

Camera on Rose checking if they have left.

Camera on the area where the guard was from Rose's perspective. There is nobody around.

Cut to Rose moving a blank of wood and entering the woodpile.

Elliot places the timber that was moved, back on the top.

Cut to Elliot and Rose kissing and embracing tightly.

ELLIOT

(Quietly) **You made it.....**

Cut to Elijah in the corner of the shack. His eyes are partially open, and he is smiling at the young re-united lovers.

Cut to Rose and Elliot. Rose is sleeping and resting her head on Elliot's chest. Elliot is deeply entrenched in his own internal thoughts.

YOUNG ELLIOT: NARRATION

It was great to have Rose back in my arms....... But the job wasn't even half done.

Cut to a shot of Elliot staring out of the woodpile through the gaps.

YOUNG ELLIOT: NARRATION

Now we just had to wait, and hope we remained undetected.

Cut to a shot of the gaps within the structure from Elliot's perspective.

Cut to the next scene.

Scene 25

EXT. NEW CONSTRUCTION SITE - DAY

Cut to a shot of the trio asleep, in the makeshift abode. Like any other day the prisoners are busy working on the site.

Cut to a shot of Fritz grappling with guards. This is seen from the trio's perspective through the gaps in the pile.

FRITZ

(Screaming) **Get off me........** *(In German: Subtitles in English)*

Cut to Elliot abruptly waking from his sleep. He peers out of the timber stack.

Cut to a shot of the outside scenes from Elliot's view. Fritz is right next to the woodpile, guards are endeavouring to take him somewhere. However, the Kapo is resisting and fighting them off.

Cut to a shot of Elijah and Rose. The fear factor has set in once again. The barks of dogs are heard.

Cut to dogs barking at the woodpile where Fritz is. One of the creatures runs towards the heap, continuing to bark. It appears to the guards that he is barking at Fritz and his scrap with the guards.

Cut to the dog next to Fritz and the guards, growling at them and sniffing around the pile.

Cut to a shot of the dog panting and looking into the gaps.

Cut to Elliot moving his head back.

Camera on the group inside the woodpile, who are anticipating the possibility of being caught.

Cut to a shot of Fritz being dragged away from the adapted mound by the guards. The dog resumes barking.

Cut to the dog waiting by the shack, sniffing around it.

Camera on the trio inside the heap of wood.

GUARD

What is it boy? *(In German: Subtitles in English)*

Cut to a shot of the gaps from the trio's perspective. The guard who is calling the dog begins to approach them. He stops by the pile. The dog is peering through the gaps, examining the area. It pauses and raises it's head. The powerful German Shepherd has it's eyes fixated on Elliot's.

Cut to Elliot's eyes. His breathing has become extremely deep and his heart rate has accelerated.

Cut to a shot of the dog's eyes from Elliot's perspective.

The guard gets on one knee and begins stroking the dog.

GUARD

What is it boy? *(In German: Subtitles in English)*

He stands up.

Cut to a shot of the trio from the dog's view. The guard's shadow is completely covering them.

Camera on the guard standing, from the view of the trio inside. He pauses.

Cut to a shot of the trio. They are expecting the worst. Rose is cuddling up to Elliot, overwhelmed by fear and tension.

Cut to the guard from the trio's perspective.

WOLFGANG

Over there. *(In German: Subtitles in English)*

Cut to a shot of Wolfgang looking at the guard, from the trio's viewpoint. Wolfgang directs the guard towards a noose where Fritz will be executed for his incapacity to marshal the inmates. However the trio are unaware of this.

Camera on the guard from the trio's view. He kneels down and puts a lead on the dog and they move away from the woodpile.

Cut to a shot of Elliot, Elijah and Rose, who are relieved.

Cut to the guards dragging Fritz towards the noose where he will be hung.

Cut to Fritz being led up some steps. Prisoners are being made to watch this exemplary public execution.

Camera on Fritz standing on a stool and the noose being lowered and fitted around his neck.

Cut to Wolfgang walking over to him. He stops in front of Fritz, staring into the demented Kapo's eyes. Wolfgang nods his head, signifying for the guard to kick the stool away. The guard does so.

Cut to Fritz suspended in the air. He struggles for a brief moment, shaking his arms and legs. After a brief struggle, his limbs go limp, as the rope gets tighter around his trachea.

Camera shot of the prisoners watching on in horror.

Cut to a shot of Elliot watching the event from the woodpile.

YOUNG ELLIOT: NARRATION

We were playing with fire..... In their eyes Fritz's errors were as bad as being an ancillary to the escape.......

Cut to Fritz hanging, dead.

Cut to Wolfgang and the soldiers walking away.

Cut to Elliot.

YOUNG ELLIOT: NARRATION

The two watch guards that were on duty yesterday were also executed later that day.

Cut to guards continuing to conduct searches in the woods.

Cut to old Elliot in his hospital bed, continuing to recite the story.

OLD ELLIOT

The searches continued for another two days....... We just had to sit there patiently for our moment.

Cut to Maggie and Robby listening attentively.

OLD ELLIOT

Then at eight pm.

Cut to Elliot in the woodpile, glancing at his watch.

YOUNG ELLIOT: NARRATION

On the 22nd of January 1945...............We made our move.

Cut to Elliot, Elijah and Rose preparing to get out.

Cut to a shot of the wood stack. The top blanks are removed. Elijah emerges from the structure.

Cut to the officers inside the camp. They are having some leisure time, before commencing the customary, evening, mass-persecution.

Cut to Wolfgang who appears to be extremely jovial and relaxed. He stops by a room with his entourage; some of them are female guards.

Cut to Gerhardt, who is walking away alone.

WOLFGANG

Gerhardt!

Gerhardt turns and acknowledges Wolfgang.

Cut to Wolfgang.

WOLFGANG

Come join us for a drink, before the barbeque commences! *(In German: Subtitles in English)*

The group goes into a fit of laughter.

Cut to Gerhardt. Although he is far from receptive to Wolfgang's sick and twisted humour, he remains respectful and courteous towards his superior.

GERHARDT

No thanks, Sir. Just gonna take a little stroll outside. *(In German: Subtitles in English)*

Cut to Wolfgang and the others about to enter.

WOLFGANG

**Suit yourself my boy. See you in an hour or so, when the
fun really begins.** *(In German: Subtitles in English)*

Wolfgang and the others begin entering the room.

Cut to Gerhardt turning and resuming to walk down the
corridor. He exits the back of the camp and is now where
the new construction site is. Snow is falling outside and the
flakes are beginning to settle on the ground, appearing to
bleach the brown terrain.

Cut to a shot of Elijah, Elliot and Rose from Gerhardt's
perspective. Elliot is assisting Rose in getting out of the
wooden structure.

Cut to a close up of Gerhardt watching the detainees about
to escape. He appears to be having an intrapsychic conflict
between his duties and his morals.

Cut to Rose climbing out, and the three of them running
off.

Cut to Gerhardt. He is completely frozen and is not
reacting to this. His ethics have prevailed over his
responsibilities.

Suddenly the exit door which Gerhardt walked out of swings open. Gerhardt turns.

Camera on a heavily intoxicated guard, coming out to keep him company.

GUARD

Ah Gerhardt. What a beautiful crisp night hey....... *(In German: Subtitles in English)*

Gerhardt moves towards the drunken guard and holds him back.

GERHARDT

Let's just go b........ *(In German: Subtitles in English)*

Gerhardt is interrupted by other guards beginning to come outside. Suddenly the guard's dog bolts out of the door. The rabid Doberman is growling aggressively and saliva is dripping from the animal's mouth. It runs straight towards the wood stack.

Cut to the guards and Gerhardt looking over at the dog. It is sniffing around the heap and barking.

GUARD

Wait.......! What is it boy. *(In German: Subtitled in English)*

Cut to the guards turning on their torches and rushing over to inspect.

Cut to the guards examining the structure.

Cut to a guard kneeling down, upon the discovery of a piece of ripped fabric, which was obviously caught on a bit of damaged wood.

Cut camera to the guards looking around.

Cut to the dog rushing off towards the direction of the forest.

Cut to Elijah, Elliot and Rose. They are sprinting down the whitened field, alerted to a further extent, by the pursuing dog. They turn to look back and see the animal approaching them in the distance.

Cut to a shot of the camp from their perspective. The disharmonious noise of guards being instructed by the officers is merged with the sounds of numerous dogs barking, insistently and inexorably.

Camera on Elliot, Rose and Elijah.

ELLIOT

Fuck! Just keep going.

Cut to a shot of the camp and Elliot, Elijah and Rose. They turn and run away from the tenacious dog, rapidly approaching them in the distance.

Camera on guards scurrying around, gathering their flashlights, rifles and dogs to recommence the search.

Cut to swarms of guards running out of the camp.

Cut to Elliot, Elijah and Rose. The trio appear to be slightly out of breath; however the thought of being caught is acting as their stimulus.

Camera on the forest ahead, from the trio's perspective. The sound of dogs barking is muffled by the sounds of oncoming bullets being shot from the guards' rifles. The snowfall has intensified and is making their movement much more arduous. They are evading the oncoming shells.

Cut to Rose slipping in the snow. Elliot quickly picks her up.

ELLIOT

Come on!

Rose gets to her feet with Elliot's assistance.

Cut to the trio running. The gunshots are showering the white surface.

Cut to the trio and the guards and dogs, chasing them.

Camera on the trio entering the forest.

Cut to Elijah. A bullet pierces through his calf. He drops to the ground in agony, clutching his injured leg.

ELIJAH

(Shrieking) **Aaaaaaaaaaaahhhh!**

Elliot and Rose halt their progress. Their warm breaths are seen in the bitterly cold air.

Elliot runs over to Elijah. He looks down at the wound and then turns and sees the pursuant guards and dogs, looming closer.

Cut to Elijah.

ELIJAH

Forget me. Just go........

Gunshots continue to be fired around the vicinity of the static trio.

Cut to Elliot keeping a low posture in order to evade the bullets. He puts Elijah's arm around his shoulder.

ELLIOT

Come on.

Cut to Elliot looking at Rose.

ELLIOT

(Urgency) **Go Rose..... Head beyond that gate. We'll catch you up.**

Cut to Rose, who is frozen and hesitant. She does not want to leave them.

Cut to Elliot ducking due to another wave of gunshots.

ELLIOT

Go!! Just go.

Cut to Rose running towards the gate, located deeper in the woods.

Cut to Elliot picking Elijah up.

ELLIOT

Come on.

The two continue to proceed ahead.

Cut to the next scene.

Scene 26

EXT. FOREST - NIGHT

Camera on guards with their guns elevated searching for the absconders.

Cut to a shot of the forest from an armed guard's perspective. The snow is delicately trickling down upon them.

Cut to the dogs sniffing around.

Cut to Elliot and Elijah, moving in and out of trees. Detrimentally, Elijah is growing increasingly reliant on Elliot's help.

Camera on the blood spewing from Elijah's leg and discolouring the settled snow behind him.

Cut to Elliot dragging Elijah along with him. Suddenly Elijah stops moving, thus terminating their progress.

ELIJAH

I can't go any further.

ELLIOT

Eli we gotta keep going!

Cut to Elliot who continues dragging him.

Cut to the duo. Elijah stops again, in excruciating pain.

ELIJAH

I can't..... I can't do it anymore.

Camera on Elliot and Elijah moving behind some trees and logs.

Elijah is seated with his back against a tree. Elliot rips off one of his sleeves and wraps it tightly around Elijah's wound.

Camera on Elliot looking around the forest. There are guards and dogs everywhere and it is only a matter of time until they get taken.

Cut to Elijah.

ELIJAH

Go on without me man........ Save yourself.

Cut to Elliot.

ELLIOT

Not leaving you Eli......

Cut to Elijah.

ELIJAH

Think about it. I'm dead either way..........

Cut to Elliot. He is staring at Elijah, refusing to abandon him. His loyalty and allegiance has clouded his rationality.

YOUNG ELLIOT: NARRATION

How could I leave him there......... He had become like a brother to me........

Cut to the guards getting closer to Elliot and Elijah.

Cut to Elliot.

YOUNG ELLIOT: NARRATION

I knew what was coming and I had to accept it........ I have never been scared of dying........ But the only thing that bothers me about it is the thought of leaving my loved ones behind.......

Cut to a shot of Rose in the fields of gold.

Cut to a shot of Elliot kneeling in front of Elijah.

YOUNG ELLIOT: NARRATION

I knew I'd never see her again..... But I just hoped she'd got away......

Cut to a side shot of the guards moving towards the submissive duo. Elliot has his head down and his hands placed upon them.

Cut to the next scene.

Scene 27

EXT. FOREST - NIGHT

Cut to a shot of Rose moving through the forest cautiously. She is looking around wondering where Elliot and Elijah are.

Cut to a shot of the forest.

Camera on Rose moving ahead. Suddenly, a low flying bird swoops down from the trees, causing Rose to duck, catching her off guard.

Cut to Rose proceeding ahead into the darkness. This is accompanied by the hooting of owls. Rose is petrified and is constantly looking around and over her shoulder.

Cut to Rose's fearful eyes. She hears some rustling coming from some bushes that she has just traversed.

Camera on Rose turning slowly.

Cut to the bush.

Cut to Rose.

ROSE

(Quietly) **Elliot?**

Cut to the bush, which stops rustling.

Camera on Rose. She turns and keeps moving ahead. The obscurity of the woodlands is clearly making Rose feel perturbed.

Cut to a shot of Rose. She moves passed the camera. The camera is now on the dark and hostile surroundings. The screen turns black.

Cut to the next scene.

Scene 28

INT. CONCENTRATION CAMP - NIGHT

The screen remains black for a few seconds. The sound of militant marching is heard.

Cut to Elliot. He is in a barrack with women, children and some frail old men. The door is unlocked.

Cut to guards entering and beginning to strip down women. The shrieking of the women echoes throughout the camp.

Camera on Elliot looking on in horror.

Camera on a woman, clinging onto her child and refuting to strip. Her child is pulled away and she is struck to the ground. The child screams.

Cut to a malnourished old man, who is being stripped.

Camera on Elliot watching on in dismay.

Cut to an outside shot of the "Little White House" and the naked people being led to it. The helpless prisoners are lined up in queues.

Cut to Wolfgang and a reluctant Gerhardt walking over to the infamous room. Elijah is being dragged by two officers to the front of the queues, where Wolfgang awaits him.

The guards stop, but carry on holding Elijah up. Wolfgang and Elijah are now facing each other. Wolfgang walks over to him and strikes him in the face. Elijah is rocked back by the intensity of the punch. The guards prevent him from falling by holding him up.

Cut to Gerhardt who feels immense sympathy for Elijah. The crowds of people are lamenting and crying in anticipation of their persecution.

Camera on Wolfgang who turns to face his audience.

WOLFGANG

Silence!!!! *(In German: Subtitles in English)*

The noise levels diminish substantially.

Camera on a women sobbing.

Cut to Wolfgang turning towards Elijah.

WOLFGANG

You have transgressed the rules of the camp..... *(In German: Subtitles in English)*

Cut to Elijah being held up, he is bleeding from the nose.

Camera on Wolfgang.

WOLFGANG

The usual punishment is public hanging...... But for you........... I'll make an exception. *(In German: Subtitles in English)*

Wolfgang pulls out a gun and leisurely shoots him in the head. Elijah drops down dead, falling near a young woman and her child.

Cut to the child and woman. They are crying uncontrollably and have moved slightly out of line. One guard slaps the woman in the face.

GUARD

Get back in line!!!! *(In German: Subtitles in English)*

Cut to Gerhardt rushing over to the aggressor.

GERHARDT

Get off her!!! *(In German: Subtitles in English)*

Gerhardt turns him around and clouts him across the face.

Cut to the guards and officers wrestling Gerhardt. They eventually throw Gerhardt to the ground. The snow dampens the back of his garments. He then gets up and walks away conveying deep anger.

Cut to Wolfgang.

WOLFGANG

Where are you going???!!! *(In German: Subtitles in English)*

Cut to Gerhardt walking away from the location.

Cut to Wolfgang and a guard standing by him. The guard goes to follow Gerhardt. Wolfgang holds him back.

WOLFGANG

Leave him. *(In German: Subtitles in English)*

Wolfgang looks over at the guards and officers. He nods his head, indicating for them to initiate the process.

Camera on a guard signifying his agreement to Wolfgang's orders by nodding his head.

Cut to the people being led into the chamber.

Camera on the last few victims entering. The door is sealed behind them. Screams and cries emanate from the room.

Cut to Wolfgang.

WOLFGANG

(Callously) **Release them.**................ *(In German: English subtitles)*

Camera on the outside of the chamber. The sounds of gas and screaming augment.

Cut to a close up of Elliot. The sounds can be heard from his barrack.

YOUNG ELLIOT: NARRATION

The sound of desperate people being tortured to death resonated around the camp........

Cut to the next scene.

Scene 29

INT. GERHARDT'S OFFICE - NIGHT

Gerhardt is sitting by his desk, with his shirt undone, drinking whiskey. His door opens. Wolfgang walks over to his desk.

Cut to Wolfgang from Gerhardt's perspective.

WOLFGANG

Mind if I join you? *(In German: Subtitles in English)*

Wolfgang picks up a spare glass on the table and pours some whiskey into it. He then sits.

Cut to Gerhardt from Wolfgang's view, who is just staring at him. There is utter silence in the room.

Camera on Wolfgang, who drinks the whiskey.

WOLFGANG

Quite a scene you caused out there...... *(In German: Subtitles in English)*

Cut to Gerhardt, who remains silent.

Camera on Wolfgang. He picks up the bottle and pours himself another glass.

Camera on the bottle going towards Gerhardt's glass. Gerhardt pulls it away.

Cut to Wolfgang looking at Gerhardt, anticipating him to talk.

Camera on Gerhardt.

GERHARDT

(Bitterly) **I have watched innocent people being; beaten, tortured, raped and murdered in the most grotesque and inhumane fashion for years....... I'm not going to be a part of this anymore.** *(In German: Subtitles in English)*

Camera on Wolfgang who chuckles and has a sip of his drink. He breathes out deeply.

WOLFGANG

(Coldly/ Quietly) **Let me tell you something.... These people are the decay of western civilisation... Vermin! Not worthy of the air they breathe.......** *(In German: Subtitles in English)*

Wolfgang becomes infuriated and greatly animated.

WOLFGANG

(Loudly) **We are doing a favour to humanity getting rid of them!!! We are on route to creating the Übermensch..... We are purifying the gene pool, so one day; we will have the master race!** *(In German: Subtitles in English)*

Cut to Gerhardt.

GERHARDT

Master race? *(In German: Subtitles in English)*

Gerhardt shakes his head to indicate his utter disapproval.

GERHARDT

You ignorant little man. You are so blinded by HIS notions. Master race? It doesn't exist...... No matter what; colour, creed, religion or sex we are all God's children.... The variety and diversity of people and cultures is what makes the world beautiful and interesting. Moreover, HE has grossly misconstrued and manipulated Nietzsche's concept in order to satisfy his own sadistic plans and visions. *(In German: Subtitles in English)*

Cut to Wolfgang looking at Gerhardt in a rage.

Cut to Gerhardt. He is the personification of composure.

GERHARDT

(Sarcastically) **Let's analyse this Übermensch, HE speaks of. Diversity and defects is what makes us great. Isn't it?**
(In German: Subtitles in English)

Cut to Wolfgang looking on perplexed.

Cut to Gerhardt.

GERHARDT

Let's take Michelangelo for example? The geniality, precision and sheer immensity of his art work stemmed from his feminine tendencies. This defect, as HE defines it and peculiarity is what enabled him to compose his great artistic creations and be immortalised. (*In German: Subtitles in English*)

Cut to Wolfgang. He is digesting Gerhardt's words and is feeling extremely uncomfortable.

Cut to Gerhardt.

GERHARDT

Our own Friedrich Wilhelm Nietzsche. Yes, a genius. Yes, a pioneering philosopher. But.............. (*In German: Subtitles in English*)

Gerhardt pauses.

Cut to Wolfgang looking on absorbing every premise of the argument.

Camera on Gerhardt.

GERHARDT

He was predisposed to mental illness and ended up spending the remainder of his days in a psychiatric ward......... Humanity is defective...... Abnormalities and differences is what makes us great. You can tell HIM, from me to revise his notions of the Übermensch. *(In German: Subtitles in English)*

Cut to Wolfgang. He slams his fist on the desk and rises to his feet.

WOLFGANG

(Screaming) **No!!! I've heard enough of your fallacies. Shame on you! Our people would die for their nation. You are a disgrace to your motherland, betraying your own kind.** *(In German: Subtitles in English)*

He pulls out a gun and points it at Gerhardt.

Cut to Gerhardt. He chuckles and then pours himself some whiskey. He has a drink.

GERHARDT

You thick bastard............. Not all of us want this...... But you are right about one thing. *(In German: Subtitles in English)*

Cut to Wolfgang aiming the gun at Gerhardt and shaking.

Cut to Gerhardt.

GERHARDT

I'm not dying for a nation....... I'm dying for humanity. *(In German: Subtitles in English)*

Cut to Wolfgang who stares at Gerhardt. In a rage he pulls the trigger, killing Gerhardt.

Cut to the next scene.

Scene 30

INT. BARRACKS - NIGHT

Elliot is seated, with his head down, alone in the barrack. The door is opened. Elliot has a quick glance over, and then looks down again.

Cut to Wolfgang and two guards walking over to him.

Camera on Wolfgang who is standing over Elliot.

Camera on Elliot. He slowly moves his head up, until he makes eye contact with Wolfgang.

Camera on Wolfgang and the two guards standing behind him.

WOLFGANG

Don't worry; I will talk in English......... I want you to understand every word of this.

Cut to a side shot of Wolfgang and Elliot. Wolfgang kneels down on one knee. The two men are face to face.

WOLFGANG

So you.... *(Pause)* You are the resilient one?

Cut to Elliot, who remains quiet.

Cut to Wolfgang.

WOLFGANG

Quite a stunt you guys tried to pull. Very..............

He pauses and looks above at the ceiling.

WOLFGANG

What's the word I'm looking for????

He looks back down at Elliot.

WOLFGANG

Very creative......

Wolfgang is smiling.

WOLFGANG

You are probably wondering why you have the privilege of my visit today.

Camera on Elliot sitting silently.

Camera on Wolfgang.

WOLFGANG

I come here as the bearer of good news. I wanted to tell you personally that your friend has been dealt with accordingly.

Cut to Elliot who is expressing profound sadness.

Cut to Wolfgang. He stands up.

WOLFGANG

Don't look so sad..... You really thought you would just waltz out of here, using your deceptive and cunning nature, which may I add is typical of your kind. You are also probably wondering why you are still alive; you know the usual sanction is immediate execution. But don't worry shooting or hanging you, would be too sudden...... I want you to suffer for days..... And if you last, for weeks.......

Wolfgang steps back and orders the guards to pick Elliot up.

Cut to the guards picking Elliot up.

Cut to Wolfgang.

WOLFGANG

Oh before I forget. She had a great disguise...

Cut to Elliot his expressions of sorrow have transformed into looks of irrepressible ferocity. The realisation that Rose is dead is a reality too harsh for him to accept.

Wolfgang moves closer.

WOLFGANG

Was it your idea?

Elliot smacks him in the face. The guards intervene and ruthlessly beat Elliot to the ground. Wolfgang kicks him in his abdomen. They stop assaulting him.

Cut to Wolfgang, he looks at the guards.

WOLFGANG

Take him away! *(In German: Subtitles in English)*

Cut to the next scene.

Scene 31

INT. CONCENTRATION CAMP - NIGHT

Elliot is being dragged down a corridor, battered and bruised.

Cut to Wolfgang opening a claustrophobic stand up cell. The guards throw Elliot in. The cell is closed.

Cut to Elliot in this small and compact, confined area. His only source of light is a little opening in the wall. He peers out at the night sky.

Cut to a shot of the night's sky from Elliot's view. The stars are sparkling.

Cut to Elliot. Tears roll down the cheeks of the devastated and beaten young man.

Cut to the next scene.

Scene 32

INT. CELL - AFTERNOON

Credits read "**January 27, 1945**".

Camera on Elliot in the cell. His eyes have massive black bags around them, his breathing is strained, and his face is as pale as a ghost.

YOUNG ELLIOT: NARRATION

I was locked in that tiny cell without food or water for days..... Left there to die of starvation.........

Suddenly sounds of gunshots are heard. Elliot assumes it is a revolt of the camp prisoners, causing the SS officers to take drastic measures. It is around 5 o'clock in the afternoon, but the darkness has already set in on this freezing cold winter's day. He hears the sounds of military boots scurrying towards him. His cell door flings upon. A severely fatigued Elliot looks up at two robust men wearing ushankas, and different military uniforms to that of the Germans.

Cut to the men.

SOVIET SOLDIER 1

Quick, we don't have much time. *(In Russian: Subtitles in English)*

They quickly help Elliot up and rest Elliot's arms on their shoulders. Although Elliot could not understand the German language or talk it, he could detect that they were not speaking it.

Cut to Elliot and the Soviet troops moving away from the cell. Whilst this is happening, other Soviet soldiers begin to shoot the guarding SS officers.

Camera on the soldiers liberating other prisoners.

Camera on Elliott and his guides leading him up the stairs to the main part of the camp where there is open fire.

Cut to a shot of the trio at the door. The shooting continues to be exchanged between the Germans and Soviets. They quickly shield Elliot from the warzone by one of them quickly dragging him into the room that they were just about to exit from.

Cut to one of the Soviet troops running out of the exit and swiftly diving behind a sheltered area consisting of wood logs.

Cut to the soldier taking cover, whilst he is showered by oncoming bullets. He waits till the firing diminishes momentarily.

Cut to the German guards reloading their guns.

Cut to the Soviet soldier. He gets onto his feet and fires at the German guards killing them, while they are trying to reload their rifles.

Camera on the other USSR soldiers rescuing people from their barracks.

Cut to the Soviet rescuers surrounding the Germans who have surrendered to them.

Cut to the soldiers leading Elliot out towards the main entrance. They stop and look down at Wolfgang.

Cut to Wolfgang on the floor. There is a soldier standing over him, pointing a gun at the tyrannical leader. Wolfgang has his hands up, pleading for his life.

WOLFGANG

(Scared) **Please don't kill me.......... I surrender........ I surrender.** *(In German: Subtitles in English)*

Cut to one of the soldiers, who rescued Elliot. He walks over to his fellow troop and signals for him to kill Wolfgang.

Cut to Elliot and the two men walking off.

Camera on Wolfgang pleading more and holding his hands in front of his face.

Cut to the Soviet soldier. He keeps a straight face and shoots him in the head, without any remorse.

Cut to Wolfgang, laying dead.

Camera on Elliot being led out of the camp.

Cut to Elliot being put in a tank and wrapped in a blanket in order to keep him warm. The snow continues to fall heavily and settle, as thousands of people exit from the hellish dwelling. (Music: The Farmer by Mike Beever).

Cut to scenes of joy as mothers are reunited with their children. The tears are now only those of happiness. Freedom and hope awaits these people.

Cut to Elliot who is seated. As the vehicle drives away, he continues to look at the death camp, completely consumed by his internal thoughts, thinking about everything he experienced in there.

Cut to a shot of the camp from Elliot's view.

YOUNG ELLIOT: NARRATION

My liberation felt like defeat not victory. I'd lost the love of my life...... I didn't want to go on. The camp may have not killed me, but my soul was dead.

Cut to a shot of Rose in the cornfields smiling.

Cut to Elliot in the tank.

YOUNG ELLIOT: NARRATION

She was gone forever.

Cut to a shot of the now distant concentration camp from Elliot's perspective.

Cut to the next scene. (Music stops).

Scene 33

INT. SHELTERED AREA - DAY

Cut to Elliot in a shelter with predominately people from the USSR. He is demolishing some food, masticating it, uncontrollably.

Camera on one of the Soviet soldiers who saved him. He walks over to Elliot.

SOVIET SOLDIER 1

I see you're enjoying your food? *(In Russian: Subtitles in English)*

Cut to Elliot who momentarily stops eating. He looks around, at the people surrounding him. He does not understand what the soldier has said and thus he responds by smiling. Elliot then resumes eating.

Camera on the soldier. He smiles and laughs, realising that he does not comprehend his language.

SOVIET SOLDIER 1

You don't understand me do you? *(In Russian: Subtitles in English)*

Camera on Elliot. He stops eating, looks around perplexed, and then nods his head and smiles.

Cut to the Soviet people laughing.

Cut to Elliot smiling and looking around confused.

YOUNG ELLIOT: NARRATION

I didn't understand a word they were saying....... But I just laughed and smiled.

Cut to the next scene.

Scene 34

EXT. CORNFIELDS - DAY

Cut to a rejuvenated Elliot being dropped off by Soviet allies at the cornfields, before his house.

YOUNG ELLIOT: NARRATION

I spent around 3 months there being catered for and looked after..... News had just gone around that the Germans had surrendered and the war was finally coming to an end.

Cut to Elliot leaping off the vehicle. He turns and looks back at the troops in the tank.

ELLIOT

Thank you. *(In Russian: Subtitles in English)*

Cut to Elliot beginning his walk through the cornfields. (Music: Adele - Someone Like You *'Instrumental'*).

Cut to a shot of the fields. It is a warm spring day. The light wind is blowing on the golden crops causing them to dance.

He proceeds walking through the fields reminiscing about Rose.

Cut to Elliot stopping. He stares at the washing line.

Cut to a shot of the washing line.

Cut to Elliot. He looks away and enters the house. He walks through and picks up the photo.

Camera on the picture of Elliot and Rose.

Cut to a shot of Elliot. He is staring at it and is becoming teary. He eventually composes himself and puts the photograph in his pocket.

Cut to Elliot getting back into the vehicle with the troops, who waited for him. As the car moves away he focuses on the mesmeric cornfields.

Cut to a long shot of the cornfields. (Music subsides).

Cut to the next scene.

Scene 35

INT. HOSPITAL - NIGHT

Scene opens to old Elliot laying in his hospital bed.

Cut to the heart monitor that is almost at flat-line.

Camera on Robby and Maggie who are crying.

Cut to Elliot. He looks out of the window into the darkness at the cornfields. He has his final breath.

ELLIOT

She's here............

Camera on Elliot whose eyes are glazing over.

Cut to the monitor which completely stops.

Camera pans into the black and white photo of Elliot and Rose (the same one as he picked up from the house) by his bed side. The screen turns completely white.

(Music: Fields of Gold by Sting). Camera cuts to young Elliot. He jumps out of the tank, dropped off by the Soviet troops who saved him. It's a fine summer's day.

Cut to Elliot. He begins walking through the cornfields.

Camera on Rose in the distance putting the clothes out to dry.

Cut to Elliot staring at her and smiling.

Cut to Rose, who stops her activity, once again telepathically sensing his presence in the distance. A smile emerges on her face. She walks towards him.

Cut to the couple walking through the golden crops towards each other.

Cut to the lovers meeting. They kiss, embrace and walk off into the sunset holding hands.

The journey through hell and its memories were over. Rose leads Elliot through the golden cornfields on their journey through paradise.

Cut to an aerial shot of the couple.

Credits read "This film was made to remember those innocent people who lost their lives in Auschwitz".

THE END

www.ingramcontent.com/pod-product-compliance
Lightning Source LLC
Chambersburg PA
CBHW071213260626
47162CB00004B/1284

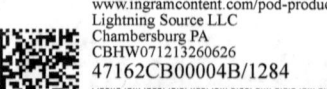